THE FASTEST RUNNER

By Eleanor Robins

Development: Kent Publishing Services, Inc.
Design and Production: Signature Design Group, Inc.
Illustrations: Jan Naimo Jones

SADDLEBACK PUBLISHING, INC.
Three Watson
Irvine, CA 92618-2767

Website: www.sdlback.com

ISBN 1-56254-685-6

Printed in the United States of America

2 3 4 5 6

The Fastest Runner

Eleanor Robins
AR B.L.: 2.6
Points: 1.0   UG

Chapter 1

Ben was in his math class. Mr. Wong was his math teacher.

The class was working on a study sheet. It was for the exam.

The next week was exam week. Ben didn't like exam week. He had to study too much. And he was never sure what the teachers would ask.

Mr. Wong was at his desk. He was going over the last test with each student.

Mr. Wong said, "Ben, your turn."

Ben got up. He walked over to the desk. Mr. Wong showed Ben his test.

Ben had an F on it. But Ben wasn't worried. He had a passing grade in the class.

Mr. Wong went over the test with Ben. He helped Ben with what he missed.

Then Mr. Wong said, "You still have a passing grade, Ben. But it is not that good. Study hard for the exam. Or you might have to take this class again next year."

Ben knew he had to study hard. But for science. Not for math. He would do OK on math.

Ben went back to his desk. He worked some more on the study sheet. But he got tired of doing it. So he didn't do it all. He was glad when math class was over.

And he was glad when school was over for the day.

Ben saw Steve after school. Steve was his best friend. They both had Mr. Reese for science. But not at the same time.

"What are you doing this weekend?" Ben asked.

"I have to study for our science exam," Steve said.

Ben said, "So do I. Do you want to study with me?"

Steve said, "Sure. As long as you really study."

"I will," Ben said.

Steve said, "I want to go out for track. Right now I have all passing grades. And I want to keep them."

Ben was going out for track too. He was the fastest runner in the school. And he had won all of his track events last year.

On Saturday the boys helped each other with science. Steve studied science on Sunday too. But Ben didn't.

Then Monday morning came. It was the first day of exam week.

Ben was on his way into the school. Steve was with him.

Steve said, "I hope I do OK. I always worry too much about my exams."

Ben thought Steve did too.

Ben's science exam was hard. But he thought he did OK on it.

Ben saw Mr. Wong after the exam. Mr. Wong was walking down the hall. He stopped when he saw Ben.

Mr. Wong said, "Don't forget what I said, Ben. Study hard for your math exam."

"I will," Ben said.

Ben would study for it. But not a lot. He had studied his science a lot. He was tired of studying. And he was sure he would do well on his math exam.

Ben studied some for his other exams. And he studied some for his math exam. But he did not study a lot for it.

The math exam was his last one. It was much harder than Ben thought it would be.

There was some math he didn't know how to do. He had been sure that kind of math would not be on the exam. So he didn't do those math problems on his study sheet.

Mr. Wong should not have made the exam that hard.

Ben was not sure he did well.

Would he still have a passing grade in the class?

Ben was sure he would.

He had to have a passing grade to go out for track.

Chapter 2

It was the first day of the new semester. Ben was in his first class. Steve was in the class too. They had history. Miss Brent was their teacher.

Ben wanted his new class card. He knew what his new classes were. But he didn't know the time of each class. And he didn't know who all of his teachers were. He just knew he had Miss Brent for his first class.

The bell rang.

Miss Brent said, "Time to start class. Get out your books."

Miss Brent always started class on time.

Miss Brent called the roll. She

wanted to make sure they were all in the right class.

Then Ben said, "Can we get our class cards now?"

Miss Brent said, "No, Ben. You will get them at the end of class. We have a lot to do now."

Miss Brent didn't like to waste time. So she kept the class busy.

But the time went by slowly for Ben. He was in a hurry to get his card.

It was five minutes before the class was over.

Miss Brent said, "You can put your books away. And I will pass out your class cards."

The class started to get ready to go.

Steve said, "I hope we have some more classes together."

"So do I," Ben said.

Miss Brent said, "Steve, here is your card."

Steve walked over to Miss Brent. He got his card and thanked her. Then he walked over to Ben.

Steve said, "See you after our next class, Ben. I can't wait for you. I want to get to class early on the first day."

Ben said, "OK. I will see you after the next class."

Steve quickly left the room.

Miss Brent said, "Ben, here is your card."

Ben quickly got his card. Maybe he could catch up with Steve. Maybe their next class was the same one.

Ben hurried out into the hall.

"Wait, Steve," Ben said.

Steve stopped. Ben quickly walked over to him.

Ben looked at his card. Then he said, "Not again."

"What's wrong?" Steve asked.

Ben said, "This is the card of the other Ben Davis. I got the wrong card first semester too. Now I have to go to the office to get my card. I get tired of that."

Ben was Ben K. Davis. The other Ben was Ben E. Davis. But he was called Ed and not Ben. Ed was his middle name.

Ben hurried to the office. He would be late to his next class. Just like he was first semester. He had to go to the office then too.

Ben got in a long line. He would have a long wait.

Ben saw Ed Davis come in the office.

Ed walked over to Ben.

Ed said, "I have your card. You must have my card."

Ben said, "Yeah. I get tired of them mixing up our cards."

The boys quickly swapped cards.

Ben knew he couldn't make it to class on time.

What a way to start the first day of a new semester.

Chapter 3

It was the next Monday. Ben and Steve were on their way to class.

Steve said, "This is the big day. We get our grades. I hope I passed all my classes."

Ben said, "I am sure you did. You studied a lot for all your exams."

Ben thought Steve always studied too much.

Ben had not studied much for his exams. But he was not worried. He was sure math was the only one he didn't do well on.

Ben didn't think Mr. Wong would fail him. But he would not know for sure until he got his grade.

Ben was glad he didn't have Mr. Wong this semester.

"I wish Miss Brent would pass out our grades first," Ben said.

Steve said, "So do I. But we know she won't. She knows we would think about what grades we got. And not about class."

Steve was right. Miss Brent waited until ten minutes before class was over. Then she passed out the grade sheets.

She called Steve's name. Steve got his grade sheet. He looked at it. He started to smile.

Steve hurried over to Ben. He said, "I did it. I passed all my classes. I can be on the track team."

"Good work, Steve," Ben said.

Ben was glad for Steve. Steve had worked hard.

Miss Brent called Ben's name. He

hurried to get his grade sheet.

Ben quickly looked at the bottom of the grade sheet. There wasn't a note that he had failed a class.

He had passed all of his classes.

He didn't look to see what his grades were. All he cared about was that he had passed all his classes. He didn't care what he got in them.

Ben walked over to Steve.

Steve said, "You don't have to tell me. I can tell from your face that you did OK. I got a B in science. What did you get in science?"

Ben said, "I don't know. I haven't looked at my grades yet. I just looked to make sure I didn't get a note."

Ben looked at his grades. They were all A's. No way were these his grades.

Steve said, "What's wrong, Ben? I

can see from your face that something is wrong."

"The office gave the wrong grade sheet to Miss Brent. These are the grades of the other Ben Davis. I have to talk to Miss Brent."

"I have to get to class. I will see you at lunch," Steve said.

"OK," Ben said.

Ben went over to Miss Brent. He told her he had the wrong grade sheet.

Miss Brent said, "You need to go to the office. Take that sheet with you. Tell Mrs. Niles you have the wrong grade sheet."

Ben hurried to the office. He didn't want to be late to his next class. He had been late to it the first day. He didn't want to be late again.

Ben went in the office. He looked for Ed. But he didn't see Ed.

Ben went over to Mrs. Niles. He was glad he didn't have to wait.

Mrs. Niles said, "How can I help you?"

Ben told her his name. He gave her the grade sheet. Then he started to tell her about the mix-up.

"You don't have to tell me, Ben. I know all about it," Mrs. Niles said.

"You do?" Ben said.

"The other Ben was here before you came. So I knew you would be here soon. And I have your grade sheet right here," Mrs. Niles said.

Mrs. Niles gave Ben his grade sheet. And he hurried out into the hall. He was sure he didn't get a note. But he wanted to make sure.

Ben looked at the bottom of his grade sheet. He had a note.

Ben couldn't believe it.

He had an F in math!

How could Mr. Wong fail him?

It wasn't fair. Mr. Wong had made the exam too hard. Now he couldn't go out for the track team. He was the fastest runner in school. The track team needed him.

Chapter 4

All morning Ben thought about the F. And it was hard to keep his mind on his classes.

Ben met Steve at lunch.

Steve said, "You don't look so good. Are you OK?"

"Yeah," Ben said.

But he really wasn't OK. How could he have an F in math?

Ben didn't want any lunch. But he had to eat something. He didn't want Steve to ask why he didn't eat.

"Did you get your grades?" Steve asked.

"Yeah," Ben said.

"How did you do?" Steve asked.

"OK," Ben said.

No way was Ben going to tell Steve about his math grade. He didn't want anyone to know he had failed. Not even his best friend.

"What did you get in science?" Steve asked.

"I got a C," Ben said.

"You could have done better. But you didn't study as much as I did," Steve said.

Ben knew that. Steve didn't have to tell him.

Steve said, "I went by the gym before I came to lunch. I wanted to see Coach Mann. But he wasn't there."

Coach Mann was the track coach. He was also an English teacher. But Ben and Steve did not have him for English.

Steve said, "But he had put up the sign-up sheet for track."

Ben didn't want to talk about track. So he tried to think of something else to talk about. So Steve would not talk about track.

Ben said, "What are you doing this weekend?"

Steve looked surprised. He said, "Why are you asking me that now? It is a little early in the week to know."

"I thought you might have some plans," Ben said.

Steve said, "I have a date with Val both nights. And we might do something Saturday afternoon. Why?"

"I was just wondering," Ben said.

"Do you have any plans yet?" Steve asked.

"No," Ben said.

"Why don't you ask Laine out? She isn't dating anyone right now. And I heard she likes you," Steve said.

"I will think about it," Ben said.

"You could do something with Val and me," Steve said.

Ben said, "I don't know. Val might not want us to do that."

Steve said, "It would be OK with her. Laine is in some of her classes. And she likes Laine OK. So ask Laine for a date."

"I don't know," Ben said again.

"Ask her to go out Saturday night. We can go to a movie. And then to get something to eat. How does that sound?" Steve said.

"OK. I will think about it. And I might ask her. I will let you know," Ben said.

He hoped Steve would not talk any more about track. But Steve did.

Steve said, "I signed up for track. Juan was there. And he signed up too."

Juan was their friend. And he had been on the track team last year. Juan was good at jumping hurdles. He was one of the best in the state.

Ben wished he could sign up for track. But he couldn't. All because Mr. Wong gave him an F in math. It was not fair.

Steve said, "I almost put your name on the sheet. But I thought you would want to put it."

Ben knew he would have to tell Steve. So he might as well do it now.

Ben said, "It is good you didn't."

"Why?" Steve asked.

"I might not go out for track this year," Ben said.

Steve looked very surprised. He said, "Why?"

"I don't want to practice every day. I get tired of practice. Some days it isn't much fun," Ben said.

Steve said, "I know. It is a lot of hard work. But it is worth it."

Ben thought so too. But he didn't say anything.

Steve said, "You have to go out for track. The team needs you. We might win all of our track meets with Juan on the team. And you."

Ben thought they might too.

"Hillman High was the best in the state in football. We don't want them to be best in track too," Steve said.

And Ben did not want them to be best. Carter High should be.

Steve said, "Think about it. Before you say you won't go out for the team."

Ben had to say something. He said, "OK. I will think about it."

But there wasn't anything to think about. He didn't have the grades. And he couldn't do anything about it.

Steve said, "Great. I know you will go out for the team."

Ben knew he should tell Steve about his math grade. But he just couldn't tell him.

Chapter 5

The next day Ben was in Miss Brent's class. Steve was there too. It was almost time for class to start.

Steve said, "Have you thought any more about going out for track?"

That was just about all Ben had thought about. And he did not want to talk about it. He wanted Steve to talk about something else.

Ben said, "I called Laine last night."

"You did?" Steve said.

Ben said, "Yeah. I asked her to go out Saturday night. I told her we would do something with you and Val."

"What did she say? Do you have a date?" Steve asked.

"Yeah," Ben said.

Steve said, "Good. I told Val we might all do something together."

Ben hoped Steve wouldn't say any more about the track team. But he did.

"Did you think any more about going out for track?" Steve said.

The bell rang. And Ben didn't have to answer him.

Steve didn't have time to ask him again when class was over. Steve had to hurry to his next class.

Ben started walking to his class. He saw Coach Mann. The coach was walking down the hall.

Ben didn't want to talk to Coach Mann. But it was too late. The coach had seen him.

Coach Mann said, "Hi, Ben. I didn't see your name on the track sign-up sheet."

"I am not going out for the team this year," Ben said.

Coach Mann looked very surprised. He said, "Why?"

"I don't want to be on the team this year. I don't want to spend all that time at practice. I just want to run for fun," Ben said.

Ben didn't want the coach to know he didn't have the grades. So he couldn't be on the team.

Coach Mann said, "You have to go out for the team, Ben. I am counting on you. I have already looked up your grades. To make sure you could be on the team."

That surprised Ben. He said, "You looked up my grades?"

The coach said, "Yes. This morning. I went to the office. And I got a copy of your grade sheet. I have it right here."

Coach Mann had a lot of grade sheets in his hand.

Then why didn't he know about Ben's F? And that he couldn't be on the team?

The coach must not have looked at his grades yet. That was why he thought Ben could still be on the team.

"Have you looked at my grades?" Ben asked.

"Not yet," Coach Mann said.

So Ben was right. The coach hadn't looked at his grades.

"I was going to look at them later in the gym. But I will do it now," Coach Mann said.

"That's OK. You can wait," Ben said.

Ben didn't want to be around when Coach Mann saw his F.

"I will do it now. I have time. This is

my planning time," Coach Mann said.

Coach Mann looked at the grade sheets. He found Ben's sheet. He looked at it.

"Now I know why you wanted me to look at your grades. I am proud of you, Ben," Coach Mann said.

That surprised Ben. He said, "You are?"

How could Coach Mann be proud of him? He had an F in math. And he couldn't go out for the team.

"All A's. Keep up the good work," Coach Mann said.

Ben could not believe it. Coach Mann had the wrong grade sheet. Coach Mann had the grade sheet of Ben E. Davis. And not his sheet.

Should he tell the coach? Or just be glad Coach Mann didn't know?

Coach Mann said, "What about it,

Ben? Will I see you at the first practice?"

Ben was still too surprised to know what to say.

"Well, Ben?" Coach Mann asked.

"I will think about it," Ben said.

"Good. I hope to see you there," Coach Mann said.

Ben was glad Steve didn't know he got an F in math.

Maybe he could go out for track. Maybe no one would find out about his grades.

Coach Mann thought he had a copy of Ben's grade sheet. No one else would look up his grades. No one would think there were two boys with almost the same name.

And Ed didn't go out for sports.

Ben should have passed math. But Mr. Wong made the exam too hard. And it was not fair.

So why shouldn't Ben go out for track?

Chapter 6

It was the first day of track practice. Ben was at the practice. Steve and Juan were there too. And so was Griff.

Griff was in some of their classes.

Steve said, "I sure am glad you are here, Ben. I wasn't sure you would be."

And Ben wasn't sure he should be there. But he wanted to be on the team. It wasn't fair Mr. Wong gave him an F.

Steve said, "I wonder why Griff is here. He didn't sign up for the team."

"Maybe he just came to watch," Ben said.

They knew Griff didn't like to do anything that took a lot of work.

Coach Mann blew his whistle.

Then the coach said, "Time for practice to start. I will call out the names on the sign-up sheet. Answer when I call your name."

Coach Mann called all the names. All the boys were there.

"Did I miss anyone?" the coach asked.

Griff put up his hand. He said, "Me, Coach."

Coach Mann looked at the sign-up sheet. Then he said, "Your name isn't on here."

"I know. I forgot to sign up," Griff said.

Coach Mann said, "I need to look at your grades. I need to know you can be on the team. I always look at all the grades before the first practice."

"That's why the coach has a sign-up sheet," Steve said.

"My grades are OK," Griff said.

Coach Mann said, "OK, Griff. You can practice today. I will look at your grades tomorrow."

"Thanks, Coach," Griff said. He had a smile on his face.

Steve looked at Ben. He said, "What do you think? Do you think Griff has the grades to be on the team?"

"I don't know," Ben said.

And he didn't care. All he cared about were his grades.

Steve said, "Maybe Griff doesn't. Maybe that is why he didn't sign up."

Ben didn't say anything.

Then Steve said, "No. Griff must have the grades. Or he would not be here. He wouldn't do that to the team."

Ben didn't feel so good.

He was glad Steve didn't know about his F.

Chapter 7

It was the next day. Ben was at track practice. Steve and Juan and Griff were there too.

Coach Mann blew his whistle. Then he checked to make sure all the boys were there. They were. But he didn't call Griff's name.

Griff said, "You forgot to call my name, Coach."

Coach Mann looked at Griff. He did not look pleased. He said, "I did not forget, Griff. I told you I would look up your grades. I did."

The coach didn't say anything else. He just looked at Griff.

Griff's face got red. He laughed. But

it did not sound like a real laugh.

Then Griff said, "It was worth a try. I thought you might forget to look at my grades."

"I never forget to look at grades. Pull your grades up, Griff. And then try out next year," Coach Mann said.

Juan said, "That does not surprise me. Griff does not listen in class. And he does not study much."

But only Ben and Steve could hear what Juan said.

Griff did not look happy as he left the track.

Steve looked at Ben. He said, "How could Griff try to do that to our team? Someone would have found out. And we would have had to forfeit every meet he was in."

Ben knew that was right. He didn't feel so good.

Maybe he should tell the coach he couldn't be on the team.

But who would ever find out there were two boys with almost the same name?

Coach Mann didn't.

Ben wanted to stay on the team. So he didn't tell the coach about his math grade.

Ben went to practice all week. And he ran some on the weekend.

On Monday he hurried to the track after school. He saw Steve and Juan. They were running around the track.

Ben ran over to them. He ran some laps with them. And they didn't talk.

Then they stopped running. It was almost time for practice to start.

Steve said, "Did you hear the news?"

"Big news," Juan said.

"What news?" Ben asked.

"About the Hillman High football team," Steve said.

"No. What about it?" Ben asked.

"The team had to forfeit its state football title," Steve said.

Ben was surprised. He said, "Why?"

Steve said, "One of the players didn't have the grades to play. He knew he didn't have the grades to play. And he still played. He didn't care about the team. He cared only about himself."

Ben did not say anything. But he did not feel so good.

Steve said, "I am glad the coach checked Griff's grades. We would have had to forfeit all the meets he was in."

Ben was glad Coach Mann blew his whistle. It was time for practice to start.

Ben hurried over to the coach. So he didn't have to talk to Steve and Juan.

Chapter 8

It was the day of the first track meet. Ben should have been very excited. He had been last year before the first meet. But he did not feel that way this year.

Ben and Steve were in Miss Brent's class. Class was about to start.

Steve said, "I can hardly wait. I think Carter High will win today. What do you think?"

"I don't know. I guess we will," Ben said.

"You don't seem excited. Aren't you excited the first meet is today?" Steve asked.

"Sure," Ben said. But he wasn't.

Maybe he would be when it was

time for the meet to start.

Ben didn't want to talk about the track meet. So he was glad the bell rang. And Miss Brent started class.

The morning seemed to last a long time. And Ben could not keep his mind on his classes. He kept thinking about the track meet.

Ben was glad when it was time for lunch. He put his books in his locker. Then he hurried to the lunch room. Steve was already there. He was sitting at a table with Griff and Juan.

Ben got his lunch. He went over to the three boys and sat down.

Steve said, "I can hardly wait for school to be over. I am ready for the meet to start. I sure am glad I made the team."

"I should be on the team. But Mr. Reese failed me," Griff said.

And Mr. Wong failed Ben.

Steve said, "Mr. Reese didn't fail you. You failed yourself, Griff. Did you study for the exam?"

"Sure I did," Griff said.

"How much did you study?" Steve asked.

At first Griff didn't answer. Then he said, "Some."

Steve said, "You should have studied more. Then you would have passed. Ben and I studied for his exam. And we passed."

Juan said, "I was worried I would fail math."

"Who did you have for math?" Ben asked.

"Mr. Wong," Juan said.

"I'm glad I didn't have Mr. Wong. He's too hard," Griff said.

Ben thought he was too.

Juan said, "He is hard. But he is a good teacher. And he is fair. Kids learn a lot from him."

"I don't want to learn a lot," Griff said.

Steve laughed. Then he said, "We know, Griff."

Juan said, "I had to study a lot for my math exam. You would not believe how hard I had to study for it. But I sure am glad I did."

Griff said, "You better be glad you did. Coach Mann checks all the grades. I didn't sign up for the team. I thought he wouldn't check grades after practice started. I thought he would forget. But he didn't."

"The coach cares too much about the team. He would not forget to do that," Steve said.

Ben didn't feel like eating. And he did not feel like talking to the boys.

Mr. Wong didn't fail him. He failed himself. Just like Griff did.

He should have studied more for the exam. Then he would have passed. And he would have the grades to be on the track team. He had only himself to blame. Not Mr. Wong.

"I have to go," Ben said.

Steve looked surprised. He said, "You haven't eaten your lunch."

Ben said, "I don't have time to eat. I forgot I have to study for a test."

But Ben didn't need to study for a test. He just had to get away from talk about track.

Ben got up. He put his tray up. Then he hurried out of the lunch room.

The rest of the school day seemed to go by very slowly. Ben could not keep his mind on his classes. All he could think about was the track meet.

Last year he had been excited about the first meet. This year he wasn't. And he knew why. He didn't have the grades to be on the team.

It was wrong for him to be on the team. It was not fair to the team. And maybe it was also not fair to him.

The end of school bell rang. And Ben knew what he had to do. For the first time in three weeks he felt good about himself.

Ben started down the hall. He was in a hurry to get to the track.

Steve was at his locker.

Steve said, "Wait, Ben. And I will go to the track with you."

But Ben did not have time to wait. He had to get to the track as soon as he could. Coach Mann would need time to pick someone else to run in his place.

Ben was the fastest runner in the school. But he would not be running for the track team this year.

Ben hurried to the track. He saw Coach Mann. He ran over to the coach. "I can't be in the track meet," Ben said.

Coach Mann looked surprised. He said, "Why?"

"I don't have the grades to be on the team," Ben said.

Coach Mann looked even more surprised. He said, "I have your grade sheet, Ben. And you got all A's."

Ben said, "But it is not my grade sheet. It is the grade sheet of Ben E. Davis."

Coach Mann said, "Why are you just telling me now? Why didn't you tell me that day in the hall?"

"I didn't want you to know I failed

math. And I wanted to be on the team," Ben said.

"But you have not been fair to the team, Ben," Coach Mann said.

Ben said, "I know. And I am sorry that I have not been."

Coach Mann said, "You should have told me then, Ben. And not come out for the team. But I am glad you are telling me now. Before the meet started. We would have had to forfeit any meet you were in."

Ben said, "I know. That is why I told you before the track meet started."

Ben was glad he told the coach about his grades. He felt better about himself. But he still wished he could be on the team.